Hugh is New

Level 6E

Written by Louise Goodman
Illustrated by Keino

What is synthetic phonics?

Synthetic phonics teaches children to recognise the sounds of letters and to blend (synthesise) them together to make whole words.

Understanding sound/letter relationships gives children the confidence and ability to read unfamiliar words, without having to rely on memory or guesswork; this helps them to progress towards independent reading.

Did you know? Spoken English uses more than 40 speech sounds. Each sound is called a *phoneme*. Some phonemes relate to a single letter (d-o-g) and others to combinations of letters (sh-ar-p). When a phoneme is written down it is called a *grapheme*. Teaching these sounds, matching them to their written form and sounding out words for reading is the basis of synthetic phonics.

Consultant

I love reading phonics has been created in consultation with language expert Abigail Steel. She has a background in teaching and teacher training and is a respected expert in the field of synthetic phonics. Abigail Steel is a regular contributor to educational publications. Her international education consultancy supports parents and teachers in the promotion of literacy skills.

Reading tips

This book focuses on two sounds made with the letter u: u as in but and u as in put.

Tricky words in this book

Any words in bold may have unusual spellings or are new and have not yet been introduced.

> ### Tricky words in this book:
>
> # Hugh doesn't fruit suits nothing

Extra ways to have fun with this book

After the reader has read the story, ask them questions about what they have just read:

How did Sue get Hugh to play?

Can you remember two words that contain the different u sounds?

> Maybe Hugh will like it if I play my ukelele and stamp my feet!

A pronunciation guide

This grid contains the sounds used in the stories in levels 4, 5 and 6 and a guide on how to say them. /**a**/ represents the sounds made, rather than the letters in a word.

/**ai**/ as in game	/**ai**/ as in play/they	/**ee**/ as in leaf/these	/**ee**/ as in he
/**igh**/ as in kite/light	/**igh**/ as in find/sky	/**oa**/ as in home	/**oa**/ as in snow
/**oa**/ as in cold	/**y+oo**/ as in cube/ music/new	long /**oo**/ as in flute/ crew/blue	/**oi**/ as in boy
/**er**/ as in bird/hurt	/**or**/ as in snore/ oar/door	/**or**/ as in dawn/ sauce/walk	/**e**/ as in head
/**e**/ as in said/any	/**ou**/ as in cow	/**u**/ as in touch	/**air**/ as in hare/ bear/there
/**eer**/ as in deer/ here/cashier	/**t**/ as in tripped/ skipped	/**d**/ as in rained	/**j**/ as in gent/ gin/gym
/**j**/ as in barge/hedge	/**s**/ as in cent/ circus/cyst	/**s**/ as in prince	/**s**/ as in house
/**ch**/ as in itch/catch	/**w**/ as in white	/**h**/ as in who	/**r**/ as in write/rhino

Sounds this story focuses on are highlighted in the grid.

/**f**/ as in phone	/**f**/ as in rough	/**ul**/ as in pencil/ hospital	/**z**/ as in fries/ cheese/breeze
/**n**/ as in knot/ gnome/engine	/**m**/ as in welcome /thumb/column	/**g**/ as in guitar/ghost	/**zh**/ as in vision/beige
/**k**/ as in chord	/**k**/ as in plaque/ bouquet	/**nk**/ as in uncle	/**ks**/ as in box/books/ ducks/cakes
/**a**/ and /**o**/ as in hat/what	/**e**/ and /**ee**/ as in bed/he	/**i**/ and /**igh**/ as in fin/find	/**o**/ and /**oa**/ as in hot/cold
/**u**/ and short /**oo**/ as in but/put	/**ee**/, /**e**/ and /**ai**/ as in eat/ bread/break	/**igh**/, /**ee**/ and /**e**/ as in tie/field/friend	/**ou**/ and /**oa**/ as in cow/blow
/**ou**/, /**oa**/ and /**oo**/ as in out/ shoulder/could	/**i**/ and /**ai**/ as in money/they	/**c**/ and /**s**/ as in cat/cent	/**y**/, /**igh**/ and /**i**/ as in yes/sky/myth
/**g**/ and /**j**/ as in got/giant	/**ch**/, /**c**/ and /**sh**/ as in chin/ school/chef	/**er**/, /**air**/ and /**eer**/ as in earth/bear/ears	/**u**/, /**ou**/ and /**oa**/ as in plough/dough

Be careful not to add an 'uh' sound to 's', 't', 'p', 'c', 'h', 'r', 'm', 'd', 'g', 'l', 'f' and 'b'. For example, say 'fff' not 'fuh' and 'sss' not 'suh'.

There is a new boy in school.
His name is **Hugh**.

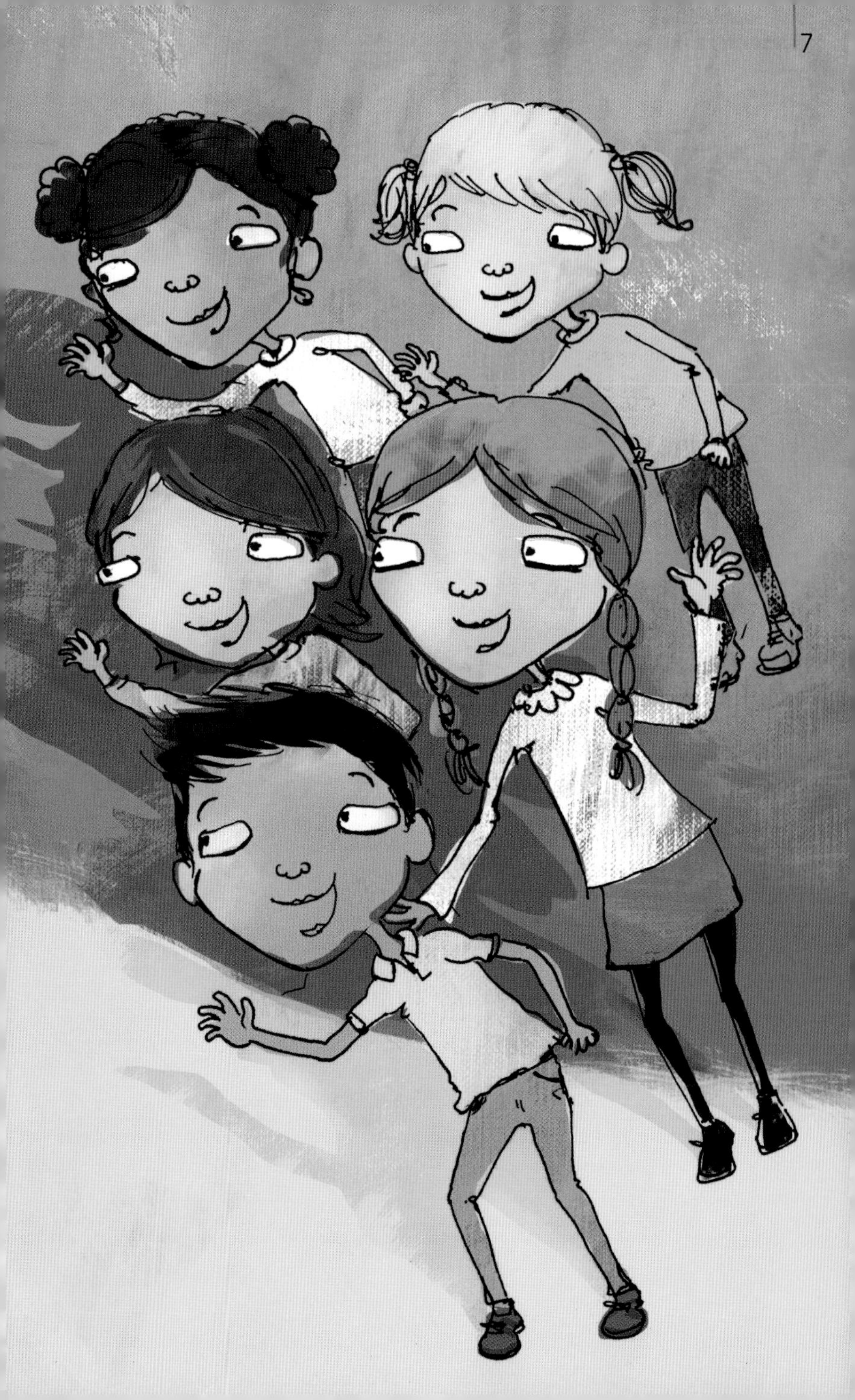

In the playground, all the kids are excited to play with Hugh.

But Hugh won't play. He stands
alone, and **doesn't** say anything.

"Maybe he's feeling blue," say the other children. "How do we get him to play with us?"

They decide the best way is to try and amuse him...

Luke and June put on a play.
Luke dresses up as a cute

unicorn and June rides a unicycle.
But Hugh doesn't say anything.

Trudy and Tallulah play a tuneful duet on the tuba and the flute.

They play the ukeleke too.
But Hugh doesn't say anything.

Ruby and Judy juggle with **fruit**
and play music on a huge bugle.

They dress up in matching
cuddly bear **suits**. But Hugh
still doesn't say anything.

"What a lot of fuss for **nothing**," they fume.

"We've tried everything and he
still won't play! That's just rude."

Then Sue has an idea. She goes over to Hugh.

"Hello, Hugh," she says. "Would
you like to play with us?"
And Hugh says...

"Yes please!"

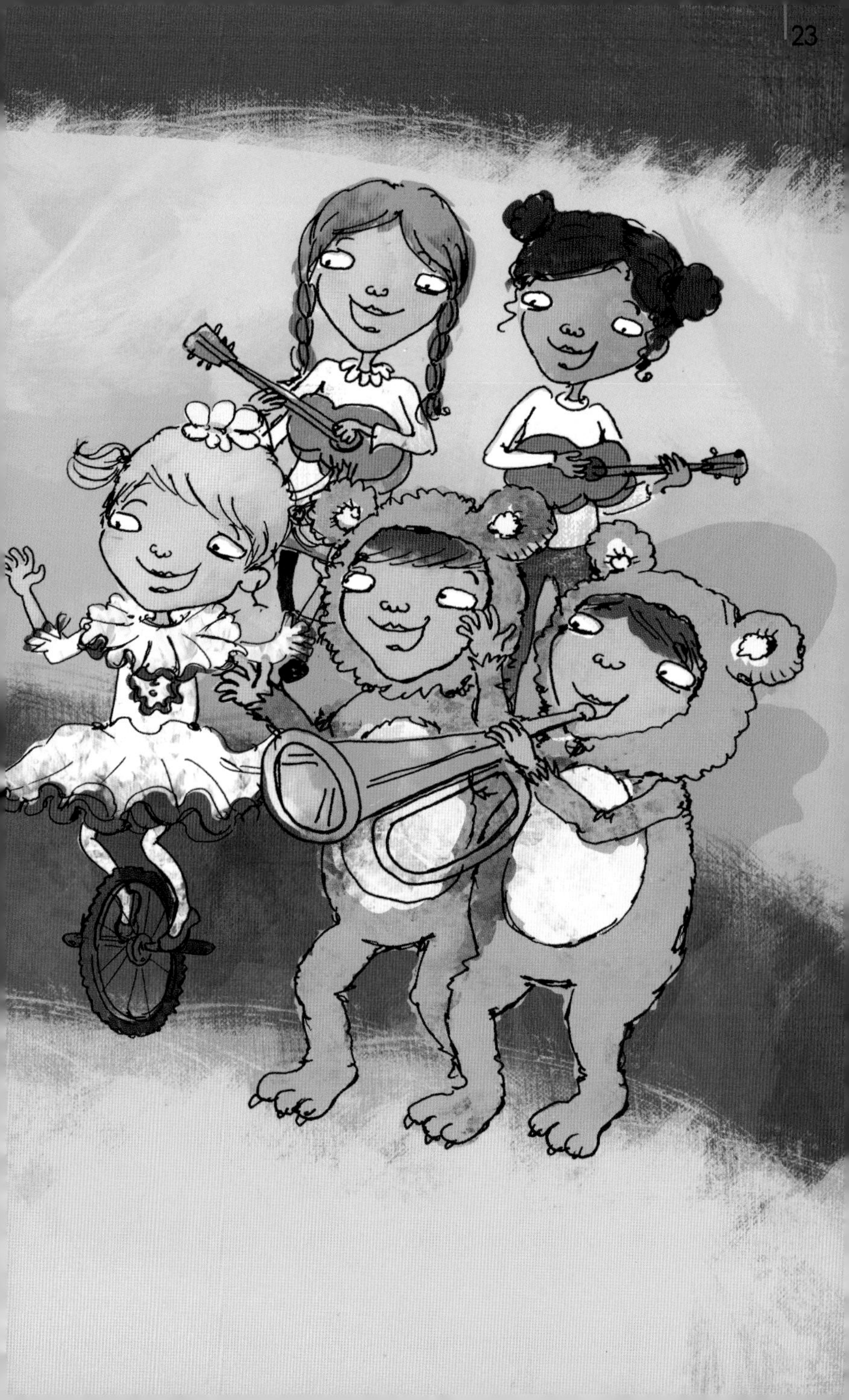

OVER **48** TITLES IN SIX LEVELS
Abigail Steel recommends...

Some titles from Level 4

I love reading phonics

The Circus Mice

978-1-84898-582-7

I love reading phonics

Monster's Night

978-1-84898-583-4

I love reading phonics

The Mummy Code

978-1-84898-585-8

Some titles from Level 5

I love reading phonics

Celebrity Celia

978-1-84898-587-2

I love reading phonics

The Cemetery Dance

978-1-84898-588-9

I love reading phonics

Goose Flight

978-1-84898-589-6

Other titles to enjoy from Level 6

I love reading phonics

Clumsy Eagle

978-1-84898-591-9

I love reading phonics

Bad Zombie Movie

978-1-84898-592-6

I love reading phonics

Owen the Astronaut

978-1-84898-593-3

An Hachette UK Company
www.hachette.co.uk

Copyright © Octopus Publishing Group Ltd 2012
First published in Great Britain in 2012 by TickTock, an imprint of Octopus Publishing Group Ltd,
Endeavour House, 189 Shaftesbury Avenue, London WC2H 8JY.
www.octopusbooks.co.uk

ISBN 978 1 84898 590 2

Printed and bound in China
10 9 8 7 6 5 4 3 2 1